A
REVELATION
in AUTUMN

A Lancaster County Saga

A
REVELATION
in AUTUMN

WANDA E.
BRUNSTETTER

BARBOUR
PUBLISHING

© 2013 by Wanda E. Brunstetter

Print ISBN 978-1-62029-146-7

eBook Editions:
Adobe Digital Edition (.epub) 978-1-62416-116-2
Kindle and MobiPocket Edition (.prc) 978-1-62416-115-5

All scripture quotations are taken from the King James Version of the Bible.

This book is a work of fiction. Names, characters, places, and incidents are either products of the author's imagination or used fictitiously. Any similarity to actual people, organizations, and/or events is purely coincidental.

Cover design: Kirk DouPonce, DogEared Design
Cover photography: Steve Gardner, PixelWorks Studios

Published by Barbour Publishing, Inc., P.O. Box 719, Uhrichsville, Ohio 44683, www.barbourbooks.com

Our mission is to publish and distribute inspirational products offering exceptional value and biblical encouragement to the masses.

 Member of the
Evangelical Christian
Publishers Association

Printed in the United States of America.

In thee, O LORD, do I put my trust:
let me never be put to confusion.

PSALM 71:1

CHAPTER 1

Bird-in-Hand, Pennsylvania

D on't push, Meredith! Don't push!" Laurie shouted as she directed her horse and buggy to a clearing along the side of the road next to an open field. The closest farm was some distance away, and Meredith didn't think there was enough time for them to get there.

A slight breeze picked up, and Meredith caught a glimpse of some fuzzy-looking dandelion seeds drifting through the air like little parachutes. The once-yellow meadow, where they'd pulled over, was now white with the globe-shaped seed bundles. One particular cycle of life was slowly coming to an end, while another's life was soon to begin.

Meredith ground her teeth together as another contraction came quickly, pulling her focus away from the dandelions. The pains were closer together, and she knew she shouldn't fight them, but it was hard to remember to breathe, like she'd been taught to do in the childbirth classes. Was it supposed to hurt this much? This certainly was not how she'd planned for her baby to be born. She'd imagined herself having plenty of warning and giving birth under the direction of the midwife at the clinic, not here in a buggy with her panicked sister, whom she was now forced to count on to help deliver this baby.

Meredith tried to remember what the instructor had told them during one of the classes, about what to do if the baby came unexpectedly at home. *"First and foremost, stay calm. Put the breathing techniques you've learned into play. Don't push prematurely. Keep your body relaxed, and work with nature."*

Struggling to deal with the pain, Meredith felt what seemed like a million emotions swirl through her brain. Her life was about to change in enormous ways. She had thought about this moment so many times, and now within minutes of this baby being born, it worried her even more. *Will I be able to do all of this on my own as I take on the role of being both mother and father? Can I provide for my baby?*

Meredith would have given anything if Luke could have been here right now, holding her hand and guiding her through each contraction. She was sure he would have remained calm and helped bring their baby into the world. Luke would have been a wonderful father. But this baby would never experience the joy of having Luke as his or her daddy.

She straightened her shoulders and drew in a deep breath. Well, Luke wasn't here, and with God's help, she would be guided along the way. First things first, though. She and Laurie would have to do this birth on their own, no matter how frightened either of them felt.

" 'In thee, O Lord, do I put my trust: let me never be put to confusion,' " Meredith quoted from Psalm 71:1. She clasped Laurie's hand tightly. "First and foremost, we need to pray and ask God to settle our nerves and guide us through this procedure."

"You're right." Laurie bowed her head. "Heavenly Father," she prayed aloud, "please give me the courage and wisdom to help Meredith bring this precious new life into the world. And I ask that You protect Meredith and the baby. In Jesus' name, amen."

"We need to gather some things," Meredith said, opening her eyes and focusing on what had to be done.

"What kind of things?" Laurie questioned, looking anxiously at Meredith. "I don't have much in my buggy and certainly nothing to help deliver a *boppli*."

"Do you have some clean newspaper?"

Laurie shook her head.

"How about a blanket or quilt?"

"There's a blanket in the backseat that Kevin and I used when we went on a picnic a few weeks ago. Oh, and there's also a large towel that I covered the picnic basket with."

"That's good. Get them, and place the blanket under me," Meredith said as she positioned herself with her back leaning against the buggy door for support.

She would have given anything to have a comfortable mattress beneath her instead of this narrow buggy seat. But during the childbirth classes, she'd learned there were far more unusual places some babies had chosen to be born. One day in the future, this would be some exciting story to share with her child.

"There's a bottle of hand sanitizer in my purse. You can use some of that to clean your hands and arms really good," Meredith told Laurie, taking control. "Since there isn't much room on the buggy seat, you'll need to stand outside with the door open so you can help this *boppli* make his or her appearance."

With her face looking a little less tense and a bit calmer, Laurie did as she was asked, and then she took her place outside of the buggy, in front of Meredith. "Try to pant, and only push very gently with each contraction," she said.

"I know. I know. But *danki* for reminding me," Meredith answered, willing herself to concentrate as another contraction came. Feeling a little less panicky herself, she was glad her sister sounded more in control. Hopefully between the two of them, they'd keep their wits and get through this without too much difficulty. Besides, there was no time to dwell on how apprehensive she felt. The baby was coming, and it was happening now!

Jonah stayed around Deacon Raber's place for a while after church, visiting with some of the men. However, when his ankle started throbbing, he knew he'd been on his feet too long, so he decided it was time to go home and rest for the remainder of the day. He needed to prop up his foot because his walking cast seemed tighter. Jonah could only assume his ankle was swelling, and the sooner he got home and off his feet, the better it would be.

Mom and Dad had come to church in their own buggy, and seeing that they were occupied with friends, he figured he probably wouldn't be missed. Besides, Jonah looked forward to spending some time alone, where he could think about his future—a future he hoped to spend with Meredith and her baby.

"Would ya like me to get your *gaul* and hitch him up to your buggy?" Meredith's twelve-year-old brother, Stanley, asked when Jonah headed for the corral where he'd left his horse.

"I appreciate the offer," Jonah said, smiling at the boy, "but Socks is a bit spirited, so he might be hard to catch."

"That's okay. I'm sure I can manage." The child grinned up at him, looking full of confidence. "Besides, with your foot still in that walkin' cast, it'd probably be hard for you to catch him."

"You might be right about that." Jonah smiled. "So if you feel up to the challenge, go right ahead."

Stanley hurried off toward the corral, while Jonah stood near his buggy. To his surprise, the boy showed up a few minutes later, holding Socks's lead rope in one hand, while the horse followed obediently behind.

"Here ya go," Stanley announced. "I got him for ya, just like I said I would."

Well, would ya look at that? Jonah thought. "I appreciate your efforts. Did he give you any trouble?"

Stanley shook his head. "After I showed him a lump of sugar, he followed me like a *hund*. I remember Luke sayin' how that always worked for him."

Jonah chuckled. Over the last few months, Socks had tamed down quite a bit. He seemed to have accepted Jonah as his new master, but the horse had never followed him like a dog. "Guess I'll have to get some sugar cubes and carry them in my pocket," he said, taking the lead rope from Stanley.

"Want me to hitch him to your buggy?" the boy asked, seeming eager to please.

Jonah was on the verge of telling Stanley not to bother, when he remembered what the bishop had said during his message. The sermon had been about servanthood and how folks should not only help others when they saw a need but be willing to accept help, too. "If we don't accept help when it's offered to us, we're being prideful," the bishop had said. "We also steal that person's blessing if we reject their help, for it is truly more blessed to give than receive."

"*Jah*, sure, go ahead and hitch Socks up,"

Jonah said. "I'll just wait inside the buggy till you have him ready to go."

Stanley flashed him a wide smile and led Socks around to the front of the buggy. While he worked at getting the horse hitched, Jonah limped around to the right side of the buggy and climbed into the driver's seat, yearning to get the weight off his feet.

Someday, when I have kinner of my own, I'll be teaching them to do things like this, he thought, watching to be sure Stanley did everything just right.

An image of Meredith flashed into his head. *If I'm ever fortunate enough to make Meredith my wife, I wonder how many children we'll have and if they'll have my dark curly hair or be blessed with Meredith's beautiful strawberry-blond hair. Would our daughters have Meredith's sweet personality? Would the boys want to learn the trade of buggy making from me?*

It was foolish to daydream like this, but he couldn't seem to help himself. He'd fallen hopelessly in love with Meredith and wanted nothing more than to make her his wife. Realistically, though, it was too soon for him to even hint at such a thing to Meredith. Her husband had been gone nearly six months, but she was still in mourning. If Jonah expressed his feelings to her, and she reciprocated, they'd have to wait to be married until she set her black mourning clothes aside after Luke had been gone a year.

Guess that's really not so long, Jonah told himself. *It's just a little over six months from now, so I'll take one day at a time and try to be patient. I'll keep helping Meredith whenever I can, and wait to see what develops between us.* The friendship Jonah and Meredith shared had been special when they were in Florida years ago, but for him, at least, recently their friendship had grown even deeper. Meredith was precious to Jonah, and for now, difficult as it was, loving her secretly was enough. Someday, he hoped, she would love him equally.

"Socks is ready to go!" Stanley called, disrupting Jonah's thoughts.

"Danki. You did good." Jonah waved and directed Socks up the driveway and onto the main road. Looking back, he saw Stanley's smile spread from ear to ear, making him glad he'd let the young boy help him.

Riding down the road, Jonah relaxed and let Socks take the lead. As they passed a field, he noticed how the dandelions had gone to seed and realized that the season was approaching an end. He thought about how he'd always liked the months during springtime and how ever since he could remember, his mother would pick tender dandelion sprouts every March. After washing them several times, she'd mix them with a little onion and cooking oil. Jonah usually ate so much his mouth would turn dry, but he didn't care. For a couple of weeks each year, Jonah's family enjoyed this special springtime salad. Sometimes, Mom cooked the dandelions and drizzled bacon-flavored dressing over them. But as far as Jonah was concerned, there was nothing like eating it freshly picked. It not only tasted good, but as Mom had often told him, the dandelion weed was full of healthy vitamins.

Jonah had only made it halfway home when he spotted a horse and buggy along the side of the road. After a second look, he realized the rig belonged to Meredith's sister Laurie, so he pulled over next to the field to see if there might be a problem.

I wonder what's going on. Jonah didn't see anyone at first, and then he spotted Laurie standing outside the buggy with the door open.

He tied Socks to a nearby tree then reached up to scratch where a dandelion seed had tickled his nose as it slowly wafted by in the breeze. Seeing that Laurie's horse hadn't been tied, he secured it, too. Then, hobbling toward the buggy, he called, "Is everything all right in there?"

Laurie turned to him with a panicked expression. "Meredith's boppli is about to be born. Could you get us some help?"

Jonah stood a few seconds, letting her words sink in; realizing the seriousness of the situation, he said, "I'll find the nearest phone shack and call 911."

Untying his horse and stepping back into his buggy, Jonah got Socks moving at a fast trot as he headed for the next Amish farm down the road. He barely took notice that his cast felt even tighter, making his ankle throb all the more. *Dear Lord,* he silently prayed, *please be with Meredith right now, and if help doesn't arrive before the boppli is born, let the birth go smoothly for both the mother and her child.*

"Oh, Meredith," Laurie said with a catch in her voice, "I don't think this boppli's gonna wait until help arrives. I can see the baby's head already!"

Meredith felt a mixture of excitement and trepidation. As anxious as she was to hold her baby, she feared something might go wrong during the delivery. Neither she nor Laurie had ever delivered a baby before, but they had the knowledge of what to expect and had witnessed puppies and kittens being born. But that wasn't the same as delivering a baby on the front seat of an Amish buggy instead of in a sterile delivery room.

"Put your hands in front of the boppli's head, and let it come out nice and slow," Meredith instructed, trying to keep her voice calm and reassuring, even though she was anything but relaxed.

"I know. The baby's supposed to slide out slowly, in waves, as your uterus contracts."

Laurie sounded more confident, as though remembering the things they'd been taught in the classes. "Don't push too hard, Meredith; just pant and push gently until the baby's head is fully out. You're doing great so far."

Meredith did as her sister told her to do. "You're doing pretty good yourself, Laurie," she said, hoping to offer encouragement. Trying to control her breathing as another contraction knifed through her, Meredith bit down on her lip, ignoring the metallic taste of blood, knowing that soon she'd be holding her precious baby.

"The baby's head is out now," Laurie said, her voice rising with a sense of excitement. "I'll use one of my clean handkerchiefs to wipe away the fluid from the baby's airway."

"Whatever you do, don't pull on the baby," Meredith coached. "Just guide its shoulders out. Once that happens, the boppli will slip right through the birth canal, so hold on tight."

"The boppli is out, Meredith! And guess what? It's a *bu*!"

"Thank the Lord!" Tears welled in Meredith's eyes as Laurie placed the baby facedown across her stomach, and she was able to look upon her precious son for the very first time. "Make certain his airway is cleared, and then cover him with the towel. Oh, and be sure you leave his face uncovered so he can breathe."

Laurie did everything Meredith said, and when the baby started to cry, both women did, too. It was one of the most emotional moments Meredith had ever experienced, and she felt euphoric.

"I'm going to name him Levi Luke," Meredith murmured once she was able to speak without sobbing. "He'll never get to meet his father or great-grandfather, but I want him to have both of their names."

"That's so special," Laurie said, wiping the perspiration from Meredith's forehead. "I know Luke and Grandpa Smucker would be real pleased."

The birth of a baby was one of the most natural things in the world, but to Meredith, it was a miracle—her and Luke's special gift to the world. Already, she could feel the power of love between mother and child. It was a bond like no other—one she would protect for the rest of her life.

CHAPTER 2

Meredith smiled as she gazed at her son, lying in his cradle next to the rocking chair in her living room. It was sweet of Alma to have given Meredith the cradle, and now, after months of picturing her baby lying in it, at last he was here, nestled all cozy and warm.

It had been three days since Levi's birth on the front seat of Laurie's buggy, and Meredith was grateful everything had gone as well as it had. Not long after the baby made his appearance, and thanks to Jonah's unexpected arrival, the paramedics had come and taken Meredith and Levi to the hospital, where both were pronounced in good condition and sent home the following day. Meredith's mother had insisted on coming over to help out for a few days, so Laurie would be staying at home to help Grandma care for the children. Alma Beechy had offered to stay with Meredith, too, but she'd come down with a cold and thought it would be best not to expose the baby. Mom had let it be known that she looked forward to helping out and spending time with Meredith and the baby, so Meredith figured everything had worked out for the best.

"I've never seen a more beautiful boppli," Mom said, stepping up to the cradle beside Meredith and staring down at Levi.

"Maybe that's because he's your first grand-child, and you're feeling a little prejudiced."

Mom laughed, her eyes gleaming with tears. "That could very well be. And just look at how attentive Fritz is with your son. Why, I don't think he's left that spot since you put Levi in the cradle."

"Jah, the pup sure seems to like being close to the boppli." Meredith reached down to pet the dog's head. "You've seen how he barks as soon as Levi wakes up. The least little noise the baby makes, Fritz comes to me and starts whimpering." She laughed. "I think he wants to make sure I know whenever the boppli's awake or needs my attention."

"Some dogs get jealous when a baby comes along, but it doesn't seem like Fritz is that way at all," Mom added. "It's kind of nice having a dog like that. It never hurts to have an extra guardian around, watching over you and the boppli."

"I know what you mean," Meredith agreed. "I haven't been keeping Fritz in the kennel much anymore. I feel more comfortable with him being inside—especially now that he's been with the baby these first few days and has adjusted so well." She smiled as she continued to admire her sleeping son. Levi had his father's white-blond hair; although it was still very thin. Would this child have Luke's adventurous personality, too? Or would he take after his mother, who tended to be a little more cautious about things?

Meredith's heart swelled with love as she bent to stroke the baby's soft cheek. All she wanted to do was stay close to Levi and take in everything about him—from his long, doelike eyelashes lying delicately on his cheeks to the way he held his thumbs, each hand encircling a thumb with his tiny fingers. Every day since Levi's birth, she had made little discoveries that made her cherish him even more.

Watching her son in his peaceful slumber, Meredith thought once again of how this precious little boy would depend solely on her. Could she make enough money selling head coverings to support them both? Should she seek employment outside the home once she was strong enough and felt that she could leave Levi with someone else during the days she'd be working? Meredith had thought at first that she would look for a job, but she didn't like the idea of being away from Levi several hours each day. There were so many unanswered questions. She'd just have to keep trusting in the Lord and take one day at a time.

"Would you like me to start supper now?" Mom asked, touching Meredith's arm.

Meredith smiled and nodded, aware of just how much her mother was enjoying this new role as a grandmother. "I think while you're doing that, I'll lie down and take a nap."

"That's a good idea. You need all the rest you can get." Mom gave Meredith a hug and hurried off to the kitchen.

Meredith was still a bit exhausted from giving birth, yet she felt full of excitement. But she knew she should take it slow and easy and try not to rush things, so she lay on the sofa, settled herself against one of the throw pillows, and tried to relax.

She'd only been lying down a few minutes when she heard a horse and buggy coming up the driveway. She figured whoever it was would probably go to the back door and that Mom would let them in, so she remained on the sofa.

A bit later, Luke's parents entered the room, wearing eager expressions.

"I hope it's not too soon for us to pay you a visit," Sadie said, "but we've been anxious to see the boppli and couldn't wait any longer."

Meredith smiled and motioned to the baby's cradle. "He's right over there, sound asleep." She lifted herself from the sofa and followed Sadie and Elam across the room. Then they all stood staring down at the baby.

"*Ach*, my," Sadie whispered, clasping her

hands together. "Just look at him. He looks like his *daed* when he was a boppli." Tears welled in her eyes as she turned to Luke's father. "Don't you think so, Elam?"

He bobbed his head. "Sure is a tiny fella. Don't remember any of our kinner being so small."

"That's because it's been so long since our five boys were born." Sadie turned to look at Meredith. "Have you chosen a *naame* for the baby yet?"

"Jah. His name is Levi Luke—after his father and great-grandfather."

Sadie smiled, and Meredith knew that despite the tears on her mother-in-law's cheeks, she was pleased with the name.

"Would either of you like to hold him?" Meredith asked, figuring Sadie was eagerly waiting and ready to hold Levi.

"We'd better not. He might wake up," Elam was quick to say.

"He's a pretty sound sleeper, so he probably won't," Meredith replied. "And even if he does wake up, it's okay, because I'm sure it won't take much to put him right back to sleep."

"I'd like to hold him," Sadie said, taking a seat in the rocking chair and extending her arms.

Meredith lifted the baby from the cradle and placed him in Sadie's arms. *How sad that Luke can't be here to share in this moment,* she thought as Sadie started humming to her new grandson.

Jonah whistled as he guided Socks toward Meredith's house. It had been three days since she'd given birth, and he couldn't wait any longer to pay a call on her.

When Jonah turned his horse and buggy up Meredith's driveway, he spotted two other rigs parked near the barn, so he knew she had company.

Should I stop? he wondered. *If her family is here, she might not appreciate me dropping by.*

Jonah's head told him to turn around and go back home, because he didn't want to overwhelm Meredith with too much company. But his heart said otherwise. He'd only seen the baby briefly on Sunday afternoon, when the paramedics came to take Meredith and the infant to the hospital. Now that she'd been home a couple of days, he was anxious to get a good look at her son, and if Meredith didn't mind, maybe he could even hold the little guy. Jonah loved kids and couldn't wait until he had some children of his own.

I'm here now, so I may as well go inside, he decided. *I won't stay long; just enough time to say hello and hold the baby.*

When Jonah knocked on the door a few minutes later, he was greeted by Meredith's mother, Luann. "It's nice to see you, Jonah. Come inside," she said politely.

Jonah smiled and stepped into the kitchen, which was filled with the aroma of savory stew. Luann was a friendly woman, and he appreciated her welcoming spirit. "How are Meredith and the boppli doing?" he asked.

"Quite well, but why don't you go in and see for yourself?" Luann gestured toward the door leading to the living room.

"I don't want to intrude, but I would like to say hello," Jonah said.

"I'm sure Meredith will be pleased to see

you. She's grateful you came along when you did and were able to call 911."

"I believe it must have been God's timing that led me there at just the right moment." He smiled. "Laurie did a good job helping Meredith deliver the boppli. God was with them, too."

"He certainly was," Luann agreed. She motioned to Jonah's left foot, still encased in the walking cast. "How are you getting along these days?"

"Okay, but I'll sure be glad to get this off my foot so I can start helping my daed more in the buggy shop. I've been able to do some things while sitting down, but I can't be on my foot too long or it starts to swell."

"Well, go on into the living room and take a seat."

"Danki, I will."

When Jonah entered the living room he halted. Sadie Stoltzfus sat in the rocking chair, holding the baby, while Meredith and Elam were seated on the sofa. Knowing that Sadie didn't care much for him, Jonah was tempted to turn around and head out the door. But before he could take a step, Meredith smiled and said, "It's good to see you, Jonah. I'm glad you stopped by. I wanted to thank you for getting us the help we needed when the baby came."

Jonah shook his head. "No thanks is necessary. I'm just glad I happened along when I did." He glanced over at Elam. "It's nice to see you."

"Same here," Elam replied.

Jonah turned to Sadie then. "It looks like you're enjoying holding your grandchild."

She nodded her agreement but said nothing.

Jonah moved slowly across the room and stared down at the baby. "I think he looks like you, Meredith," he said, looking back at her.

"He looks just like Luke," Sadie was quick to say.

Jonah squirmed. Since he'd never met Luke, he couldn't say whether the baby looked like his father or not. But he wasn't about to argue with Sadie. It was obvious from the icy-cold look on her face that she wasn't happy to see Jonah there, so he didn't dare ask if he could hold the baby.

How long will Sadie's hostility towards me continue? he wondered. *Will her dislike of me make it harder to win Meredith over? I wonder just how much influence Sadie has with her daughter-in-law.*

Jonah took one last look at the baby then moved across the room to where Meredith sat. "He's a nice-looking boppli. Have you chosen a name for him yet?"

She smiled. "Levi Luke."

"That's a nice name," Jonah said. "I'm sure if his daed were here, he'd be real pleased."

Tears pooled in Meredith's blue eyes. "I know he would."

"Well, I'd best be going. Just wanted to come by and see how you're doing and take a peek at the baby." Jonah started for the door but turned back around. "I should be getting my walking cast off sometime in the next two weeks, so as soon as I'm able, I'll come by to help with any chores you may need to have done."

"Don't concern yourself with that," Sadie curtly replied. "Elam and Meredith's daed will take care of any chores that Meredith might need to have done."

Hesitantly, Jonah glanced at Meredith to see her reaction and was pleased when she smiled and said, "I appreciate you coming by today, and I'll let you know if I need anything."

At least she hasn't shut me out, Jonah thought as he hobbled from the room. *I just need to make sure that the next time I drop by Sadie isn't here.*

Philadelphia, Pennsylvania

Eddie stood looking out the window of his room for one last time. He'd gotten used to the scene before him, and during his stay here in rehab, he had enjoyed watching the bluebirds come and go as they busily fed their babies inside the birdhouse. Toward the end of spring, he'd even watched as the babies left their nest, all gathering at the entrance of their little house. Then one by one, they'd taken flight, landing in the nearby shrubs. The poor parents had been frantic, flitting from one chick to the next, trying to keep them all in sight.

Redirecting his thoughts, Eddie glanced down at the pale yellow shirt and denim jeans he now wore. Susan had stopped by yesterday to give him some clothes to wear on the day of his release. She said they were a gift from her grandparents. From what Eddie had been told, he hadn't had much when he'd come to the hospital—only the clothes on his back, which he'd later learned had been so tattered they were thrown away. He shook his head slowly, wondering once more if anybody had been searching for him.

Susan and Anne's grandparents must be really nice folks. Imagine, letting a complete stranger stay with them, let alone buying me clothes, Eddie thought. The jeans and shirt fit pretty well, although for some reason he felt funny wearing them. He couldn't figure it out, but the pullover shirt felt a bit constricting, even though it fit good and wasn't tight. And the jeans, although they fit around his waist, seemed somewhat snug against his skin.

Eddie left the window and looked in the mirror across the room. Who was this person staring back at him? Even though he was dressed in normal clothes, nothing sparked a memory or a small glimpse of his past.

"Wow, just look at you! Those clothes my

grandma bought for you fit quite well," Susan said, stepping into the room. "Anne and I tried to guess your size, and it seems like it was a pretty good guess."

Eddie smiled. "I appreciate the clothes, but I'll never be able to repay your grandparents for letting me stay in their home."

"They're happy to do it." Susan motioned to the door. "Are you ready to head out?"

He nodded and grabbed the satchel the hospital had provided with his comb, toothbrush, and other toiletry items. Eddie didn't admit it to Susan, but he was a bit nervous about meeting her grandparents. What if they didn't like him? What if things didn't work out for him to stay in their home? Where would he go then?

Feeling as though he was leaving the only home he'd ever really known, Eddie squared his shoulders, ready to start another phase of his life. Maybe by being in new surroundings, his memory would come back to him.

CHAPTER 3

Bird-in-Hand

"I can't believe Jonah had the nerve to show up at Meredith's this evening," Sadie fumed as she and Elam headed for home in their buggy.

"Guess he wanted to see the boppli, same as you and me," Elam responded, holding tightly to the reins as they passed the horse farm not far from their place.

Dobbin nickered but didn't slow down when a few of the horses ran to the fence, watching as they rode by.

"But Jonah's not part of our family, and he's

pushing his way in as though he is," Sadie said with a huff.

Elam grunted warily. "You need to mind your own business. We've been over this before, and it's time you realized that Meredith has her own life to live. If her future includes Jonah someday, then you'll just have to accept it." He clucked to the horse, while nudging Sadie's arm. "See there," he said, pointing to the west. "That's what you should be enjoying instead of fretting about things beyond your control."

Sadie glanced at the sky, ablaze from the beautiful sunset. The deep orange near the horizon blended with the hues of pink and purple, making Dobbin's auburn coat glow even more. As lovely as it was, it didn't remove the worry she felt deep in her heart. Elam might be able to deal with it, but she wasn't sure she could ever accept the idea of another man taking her son's place in Meredith's life. Sadie didn't know what she was most afraid of—Jonah stepping in, or Meredith pushing them out of her and little Levi's lives. What if Meredith fell in love with Jonah and they got married? What if they decided to move away? It would be a hard pill to swallow if she never got to know her new grandson well. She was sure Meredith's mother wouldn't like it either.

"How'd your visit with Meredith go?" Jonah's mother asked as they ate supper that evening. "Are she and the boppli doing okay?"

Jonah nodded. "He's a cute little fellow, and they both seem to be healthy enough, but I wish I hadn't gone over there today."

"How come?" Dad asked, reaching for the basket of bread.

"I should have realized her family would be there. Besides Meredith's *mamm*, Sadie and Elam were there, too." Jonah solemnly grimaced. "I got a cold reception from Sadie, which made me very uncomfortable. I don't think she wanted me anywhere near Meredith or the boppli."

Mom handed Jonah a bowl of green beans. "Why not? You didn't go over there with a bad cold or anything contagious."

"I think she's still upset about me seeing Meredith," Jonah replied. "Remember when I said she'd talked to me about it?"

Mom frowned. "I was hoping she'd get over that."

Jonah shook his head. "Apparently not. She made me feel like I didn't belong there, so I only stayed a few minutes."

"How'd Meredith react to you dropping by?" Mom asked.

"She seemed okay with it; although she didn't say a lot, except that she appreciated me coming by and would let me know if she needed anything."

"Well, there ya go!" Dad grabbed a drumstick from the platter of fried chicken. "Don't think she would have said that if she didn't want you comin' over."

Jonah smiled. "Guess you're right. I'll just have to make sure that the next time I go, Sadie's not there."

"That's probably a good idea." Mom patted Jonah's arm affectionately. "As time goes by and Sadie comes to grips with her son's death, I'm sure she'll warm up to you. After all, it's not like you and Meredith are courting or planning to get married."

Jonah shoved the beans around on his plate, debating whether he should tell his folks how much he cared for Meredith. Throwing caution to the wind, he blurted out, "I'm in love with Meredith, but I won't express my feelings to her until I think she's ready."

Philadelphia

"Whew! It sure is hot this evening. I'll be glad when fall gets here and the weather turns cooler," Susan said as she pulled her compact car out of the hospital parking lot.

Eddie gave a brief bob of his head.

"Autumn's my favorite time of the year," she continued. "I love all the pretty colored leaves, but the season's colors don't last long enough for me."

Still no response from Eddie. Maybe he seemed pensive because he didn't remember the colored leaves from autumn. Or perhaps he was deep in thought and didn't hear what she'd said. "October is my favorite month; although it goes too quickly for me." Susan tried once more to engage him in conversation.

"Hmm. . ." Eddie quietly responded as he watched out the side window.

Changing the subject, Susan informed Eddie that traffic would be thinning out once they got off the expressway and headed toward Darby. "If traffic is bad, it could take us half an hour to get home, but most times it only takes ten to fifteen minutes to get to my grandparents' house." She scowled, watching as the guy who'd just passed her in a sports car cut over in her lane, way too close. "Boy, you sure have to watch people like a hawk. Just look at the way that man is weaving in and out of traffic, like he owns the road."

Eddie released a heavy sigh—almost a groan. "I still can't get over the fact that your grandparents would be willing to take me in when we've never met."

She smiled, realizing that Eddie hadn't even noticed the crazy driver whose sports car was now nearly out of sight.

Relaxing a little after they got farther away from Philly, Susan pushed the button to close the windows and turned on the air-conditioning. The cool air felt wonderful, and having the windows closed drowned out the road noise as well. Hearing that alone could frazzle one's nerves. "After you get to know Grandpa and Grandma, you'll understand," she said, glancing over at Eddie with a smile. "They're the most loving couple, and they always try to follow God's principles, while showing others what it's like to be a Christian by their actions."

Eddie squinted and rubbed his forehead. "I have no memory about whether I'm a Christian or not. But I have seen from the way you and your sister have treated me, as well as the scriptures you've read and the prayers you've said on my behalf, what it's like to show your beliefs and not just talk about them."

Susan nodded. "The Bible tells us in John 13:35: 'By this shall all men know that ye are my disciples, if ye have love one to another.' "

"Hmm. . .guess that makes sense," he said, thoughtfully tapping his chin.

Susan was tempted to say more but decided to let him think about the verse of scripture she'd quoted as they got off the exit ramp and onto the road toward Darby. She was sure that Eddie would be hearing plenty of verses in the days ahead, not to mention seeing for himself what a fine example of Christianity her grandparents lived.

Darby, Pennsylvania

When Susan pulled her car into the driveway of a large, two-story house a short time later, Eddie was impressed with the two huge maple trees in front. He was sure he couldn't reach his arms around them, their trunks were so huge. He figured the trees probably made good homes for a lot of birds, and they looked like they'd be fun to climb, too—that is, if he were still a kid. *I wonder if I used to climb trees when I was a boy.*

"Well, this is it," Susan said, turning off her ignition. "This is where my grandparents have lived since they were married. You'd never know it from the looks of all the well-maintained homes in the area, but this is actually one of the older, original neighborhoods of Darby. Their house isn't as new as some of the homes we passed along the way, but it has lots of room, and I believe you're going to like it here. Grandma and Grandpa are pretty active for their age, but I think they'll appreciate your help with some of things they're not able to do anymore."

"I'll be happy to help out," Eddie said, staring at the stately old home. "It's the least I can do in exchange for them letting me stay here."

"I'm sure they'll appreciate that. Grandpa and Grandma do a lot of charity work, and they give to others at church, too. So it'll be nice for them to be on the receiving end for a change." Susan's cheeks turned pink. "Well, just listen to me chattering away like a monkey begging to be fed. Guess we'd better go in." She opened the car door.

Just as they were getting out, an elderly couple came out of the house and met them on the sidewalk.

"Grandma and Grandpa," Susan said, gesturing to Eddie, "this is Eddie." She motioned to her grandparents. "I'd like you to meet my grandpa, Henry, and my grandma, Norma."

Henry shook Eddie's hand firmly.

Eddie smiled. *For an older man, he sure has a strong, firm handshake. I'll bet he's still pretty capable of doing a lot of the work around here himself.*

When Eddie reached for Norma's hand, she offered a welcoming handshake. Even though he'd been a little nervous about meeting Susan's grandparents, Eddie found himself instantly comfortable with these two friendly people.

"Come in. Come in." Norma offered Eddie a warm smile as she stepped onto the porch and opened the front door. "We hope the traffic wasn't too bad coming out of Philly this evening. It can get pretty snarled on that interstate sometimes."

"Other than some guy in a little sports car cutting me off, coming out of the city wasn't too bad," Susan said as they stepped into the hallway.

Once inside, a wonderful aroma hit Eddie's nostrils, and it was all he could do not to head straight for the room it was coming from.

"It's almost suppertime, and as soon

as Anne gets home from the errands she's running, we'll be ready to eat," Norma said. "I have a pot of homemade vegetable soup simmering on the stove, and we also fried up some ham to have for sandwiches."

Henry bobbed his head. "My wife made some of her famous coconut cookies for dessert, too."

Susan leaned close to Eddie's ear. "You'll never be able to eat just one of those cookies, either. Grandma's coconut dreams, as I like to call them, are so chewy and soft you'll automatically reach for more. Not only that," she added, smiling at her grandmother, "but Grandma's cookies have won many blue ribbons at the church bazaar each year."

A blotch of red erupted on Norma's cheeks. "Now there's no need to brag on my cookies, dear. After supper we'll let Eddie be the judge of how good they are."

"Don't let my wife fool ya. She's a real fine cook." Henry grinned at Norma. "I'm gonna show Eddie around the house now."

"That's good. I'll help Grandma set the table while you do that," Susan said. "Eddie, you can set your satchel over there by the stairway, while Grandpa shows you around down here."

Eddie followed Susan's grandfather to the kitchen and looked when Henry pointed to a desk in the corner. "There's a laptop computer right there, in case you ever want to use it."

Eddie scratched the side of his head. "I can't remember if I even know how to use a computer."

Henry chuckled. "Don't worry about it, son. I don't use the computer either. Susan and Anne have both tried to teach me, but that kind of technology is way over my head."

Eddie tagged along with Henry as they went from room to room and then headed up a flight of stairs. He noticed that though the house was neat and tidy, it also had a cozy, lived-in feeling.

"This will be your room," Henry said, after they'd entered the first door on the right. He opened the closet door. "As you can see, Norma got you a few more items of clothing." He motioned to the outfit Eddie was wearing. "The shirt and jeans she sent to the hospital with Susan seem to fit you quite nicely."

Eddie nodded. "Yes, and I appreciate it."

Even though the clothes felt a bit uncomfortable to him, he didn't want to sound ungrateful, so he kept that thought to himself.

"There are a few things in the dresser drawers you may find useful as well," Henry said. "Oh, and feel free to open or close the curtains whenever you want. Your room gets the morning sun, but I'm sure the birds will wake you before it's fully daylight." He chuckled. "They like to roost in the trees around here, and it's a bit of a chorus every morning when they start chirping away. We rarely set an alarm clock anymore, 'cause we're usually up with the birds at the crack of dawn. But don't feel that you have to get up early," he quickly added. "You can sleep however late you want."

Eddie couldn't remember how early or late he'd ever gotten up before his stay in the hospital. He didn't remember setting an alarm clock either. But he did look forward to hearing those birds chirping and waking him every morning, instead of all the hospital sounds he'd grown accustomed to over the last several months. He didn't think he'd miss hearing the constant voices out in the hall and at mealtime or the food carts with their squeaky wheels and rattling dishes as the nurse's aides pushed them into each room. Although the hospital food wasn't too bad, it didn't compare to that delicious smell coming from the kitchen downstairs.

Wonder where I lived before all of this. Did I wake up with the sun or when the birds started singing each morning?

"Anne's home now, and supper's ready!" Norma called up the stairs.

"The bathroom's right down the hall." Henry motioned in that direction. "Guess we oughta get washed up before we eat, or Norma might not let us sit at her kitchen table."

Eddie grinned. *These folks are sure nice. Whatever my life was before all of this, I'm pretty lucky to be here right now. Sure hope I don't do anything to mess up. I wouldn't want them to ask me to leave and then end up having to sleep somewhere on the streets.* Wherever Eddie's real home was, he hoped there was a sense of belonging like he felt here.

CHAPTER 4

Bird-in-Hand

"I can't believe your boppli is a month old already," Meredith's friend Dorine said as the two of them sat on Meredith's front porch one hot Monday morning in early August.

Meredith smiled and stroked the top of her son's silky head. "I know, and he's growing as fast as the weeds in my garden."

"I can't do anything about how fast Levi's growing, because that's what babies do," Dorine said, motioning to her own son and daughter playing on the other end of the porch. "But I can do something about those weeds in your garden."

"There's no need for you to do that," Meredith responded quickly. "Laurie said she'd pull them later this week. Today, I just want us to sit and visit. Between you taking care of Merle and Cathy, and me balancing my time between caring for Levi and making head coverings, we don't get to see each other that often."

"That's true." Dorine sighed. "Things were much easier when we were girls playing on the swings in your folks' backyard or riding around my parents' field in my pony cart." Dorine settled against her porch chair with hands clasped behind her head. "Just listen to those cicadas. When I was younger, hearing them always reminded me that school was about to start."

"Jah, it's funny how hearing certain things sparks memories." Meredith chuckled. "I'll never forget the time your daed bought that new pony and we took him out before he'd had a chance to get to know you very well. Little Rosie wouldn't pull the cart for us at all."

Dorine giggled. "That stubborn pony waited till we got out of the cart, and then she took off across Dad's field like a shot. My brother Thomas wasn't too happy when he had to chase after Rosie and bring her back to the barn." She gestured to her two little ones again. "Makes me wonder what kinds of things Seth and I will have to handle with our own kinner."

"Guess it's good that we don't know what the future holds." Meredith leaned over and kissed Levi's little nose. "If we did, it might be too hard to bear." She moaned. "When I fell in love with Luke, never in a million years did I think I'd lose him the way I did."

Dorine reached over and clasped Meredith's hand, giving her fingers a gentle squeeze. "That's why it's best to take one day at a time, asking God to give us the strength and courage to deal with things as they come."

Meredith nodded slowly. She knew her friend's words were true, but living them out was a tall order sometimes.

"On a lighter note," Dorine said with an eager expression, "how would you feel about the two of us hiring a driver and taking our kinner to the Elmwood Park Zoo the first week of September? By then the weather should be cooler. We can stop in Paoli on the way there and see the hot air balloons."

"That sounds like fun," Meredith said. "But Levi's so young yet. He wouldn't get much out of going to the zoo."

"True, but since you're nursing, you probably wouldn't want to leave him with anyone for the day."

"You're right about that, and if I go, I'll take the boppli along." Meredith's thoughts went to Jonah. The last time he'd stopped by to visit, he'd mentioned something about visiting the zoo sometime in the future. Meredith was tempted to invite him along but thought better of it. She didn't want anyone to think they were a courting couple. Besides, she and Dorine hadn't done anything together for a long time, so this day would be just for them and their children.

Darby

"What would you like me to do this morning?" Eddie asked as he and Henry got up from the breakfast table.

"Why don't you take the day off and laze around the yard?" Henry draped his arm across Eddie's shoulders. "Between your therapy sessions at the hospital and all the odd jobs we've found for you to do around here these past four weeks, I think you deserve some time off."

Eddie shook his head vigorously. "I wouldn't feel right about doin' nothing all day. You and your wife have been so kind to take me in. The least I can do to pay you back is to keep doing chores." He was glad when Henry nodded his agreement.

Eddie had settled in nicely after moving to the Baileys' house a month ago. Right from the start, Norma and Henry had gone out of their way to make him feel at home. When he'd first arrived, it hadn't taken him long to realize that he'd been worried for nothing. Anne and Susan's grandparents made sure he didn't want for a thing.

Thinking back on getting familiar with the room he'd been given that first day, Eddie couldn't believe how considerate this couple had been—especially when he had looked in the dresser drawers and found all the items

Henry and Norma had gotten for him. These kind folks had gone to the store and bought him underwear, socks, T-shirts in various colors, two pairs of jeans, two sets of pullover sweatshirts with matching sweatpants for the upcoming autumn weather, some dressy slacks and shirts to wear when they went to church, and a pair of pajamas. In the closet, he'd found a jacket for colder weather, and a lighter-weight hooded sweatshirt, as well. On the closet door hung a red baseball cap, which he'd immediately put on his head. It fit him quite well, and except for meals and sleeping at night, he wore it most of the time. On top of the dresser, he'd noticed a man's hairbrush, comb, a razor, and shaving cream. He still couldn't believe they'd thought of everything he might need.

Even after a month's time, it almost brought tears to Eddie's eyes, thinking about the kindness Susan, Anne, and their grandparents had shown him. Before he'd come here, Susan had mentioned that she'd told her grandparents about his amnesia and said she hoped he didn't mind. That didn't bother Eddie at all. He wasn't ashamed of his situation, just frustrated by it.

Almost from the start, Eddie had started healing—physically, that is. He enjoyed helping Henry with his garden, pulling weeds and seeing what vegetables were ready to pick. Overnight, the cucumbers seemed to double in size, and the warm weather was making the tomatoes turn a brilliant red. The Baileys even had a small patch of sweet corn, and just this week the ears had become ripe for picking. Norma had told Eddie that August was "produce month," and she was right about that.

Last evening, they'd all sat around the picnic table in the backyard, enjoying their first kettle of steaming corn on the cob. Eddie couldn't seem to get enough of it. Everyone laughed when George, the squirrel, ran up the tree with a cob of corn Henry had given him. Norma had also made what she called "cucumber delights," which consisted of slices of cucumber on a small piece of pumpernickel bread that had been spread with cream cheese. On top of the cucumber, she'd sprinkled some lemon pepper. Eddie couldn't believe how good they were.

The Baileys' yard was so inviting, and Eddie could understand why they liked to spend time outdoors. He liked all the trees in their neighborhood, too. They were so big along the property line that he couldn't even see the house next door. All the homes in the neighborhood weren't real far apart, but they were just close enough to run to in case of an emergency. Eddie couldn't get over how close-knit everyone seemed to be. He'd even gotten used to seeing certain neighbors waving to him as they took their daily walk down the tree-lined street.

Henry and Norma were not only hospitable in sharing their home with Eddie, but they were easy to talk to, as well, just like their granddaughters. Eddie found himself laughing more times than not as the Baileys shared some of their special memories from the past. He had to admit it felt good to find something to laugh about these days.

Norma, who'd been standing at the sink doing dishes, lifted a soapy hand and shook her finger at Eddie, bringing him out of his daydreaming. "Now you listen to my husband, young man. He's right about needing to take it easy sometimes. In fact, I insist that you take two days off every week for as long as you're staying with us. Sunday is one of them, of course, because the Lord commands us to rest on the Sabbath." Two dimples dotted Norma's cheeks when she smiled. "But you can choose which of the other days you'd rather not work, and it doesn't have to be the same day every week."

Eddie lifted his hands in defeat. "Guess I have no other choice."

Henry thumped him lightly on the back. "Now that we have that all settled, why don't the two of us head out to the backyard and relax on the porch glider for a while? Anyways, George is probably anxious to see if we have a treat for him today. When we get tired of sitting, we can take a walk around the neighborhood."

Eddie nodded agreeably. That cute little squirrel sure was entertaining, and he liked the fact that George had begun to eat from his hand, just like he did with Norma and Henry. For the first time in a long while, Eddie felt lighthearted. Although he was unsure how long it would last, he had a feeling of belonging and looked forward to each new day. It was nice to see Susan and Anne more often, too. It was almost like having a family of his own.

Eddie had energy inside that had been pent up way too long and was just itching to be used. It wouldn't be easy to sit around today and do nothing, but if it made Henry and Norma happy, then he'd do it.

Philadelphia

"I can't believe how warm and humid it is today," Susan said to Anne as they visited during their morning break, sitting on a bench outside the hospital grounds. Today was one of the few times they had the same schedule, and Susan was glad for the opportunity to visit awhile with her sister.

"I know what you mean." Anne fanned her face with her hand while blowing out, which lifted her curly bangs off her forehead.

Susan giggled. "Did you see how Eddie enjoyed the corn on the cob we had for supper last night?"

"Yes." Anne grinned. "I have to say, I think I

enjoyed it as much as he did. Corn always tastes better when it's fresh from the stalk. And it was so tender and sweet."

Susan bobbed her head in agreement. "How'd Eddie's therapy session go yesterday?" she asked.

"Real well. He's gained back most of his mobility, but as you know, none of his memory has returned. I hate to say this, but maybe it never will."

Susan sighed, remembering how last night after supper she and Eddie had taken a walk to a nearby park. They'd visited, laughed, and strolled hand in hand. Susan felt like a teenage girl when Eddie pushed her on one of the swings. She was beginning to form a strong attachment to him and thought he might be starting to care for her, too. But nothing could come of it unless he regained his memory. He might be married, and until she knew for sure that he was single, she couldn't allow herself to fantasize too much about having a permanent relationship with Eddie.

"Say, I have an idea," Anne said, nudging Susan's arm.

"What's that?"

"Why don't the two of us take Eddie on a little outing to see the hot air balloons in Paoli?" Anne suggested.

Susan shook her head. "It's too warm out for that. Besides, we won't have the same days off until the first week of September."

"That's okay. I was thinking early September. It'll be better if we go when the weather's a bit cooler."

Susan considered the proposal then said, "I think that might be a good idea. It'll be fun for all three of us."

CHAPTER 5

Bird-in-Hand

Harebscht is definitely upon us," Jonah said, blowing warmth into his hands as he and his dad worked together in the buggy shop on the first Saturday of September. "Can't ya just feel the chill in the air?"

"Jah, fall is one of my favorite times of year, and the heat from the woodstove sure makes the shop feel good this morning," Dad said, reaching for a safety triangle to apply to the back of the Amish buggy they'd just repaired. The rig had been in an accident a few weeks ago, but they'd made it look good as new.

Fortunately, the Amish family who'd been in the buggy when it had been hit by a car hadn't been seriously hurt. Many Amish involved in buggy accidents weren't so lucky.

Jonah was happy to be working with his dad again—especially since they were a bit behind. He'd only been able to help in the shop a little during the time his ankle had been broken. It wasn't fun being laid up, but they were catching up with things now. Last week, he'd been able to begin work on an antique carriage for an Englishman who lived in the area, and that task had been keeping him busy as well. The only downside was that he hadn't been able to spend as much time with Meredith and the baby lately. He'd seen them at church last Sunday, though, and noticed that little Levi was growing like a weed. It was hard to believe he was two months old already.

When Jonah had stopped to see Meredith a few weeks ago, the baby, while lying in Meredith's arms, had actually looked up at him and smiled. Jonah's heart had melted when the little guy did that, and he knew it would be hard to hide the mounting attachment he felt each time he saw Meredith and Levi. There was no stopping the images in his mind of Meredith and her son becoming a part of his family one day. Those thoughts were close to the surface almost every waking hour, not to mention the recurring dream that had recently filled his nights with hopes of the future.

Levi's going to need a daed, Jonah thought. *And Meredith needs a husband to love, nurture, and take care of her. I don't know how much longer I can wait before expressing my feelings to her.*

Darby

Eddie woke to the fresh smell of coffee and bacon. As he hurried to get dressed, he grinned, thinking if he stayed with the Baileys too much longer, he'd probably gain weight from Norma's good cooking.

That's okay, though, he thought, patting his flat stomach. *It probably wouldn't hurt for me to put on a few extra pounds.* As he bent his arm and made a fist, Eddie decided that he liked the larger muscles he'd recently noticed. It was wonderful to be healing and feeling better every day. Likewise, it was satisfying for Eddie to have a routine, even though things weren't altogether perfect. Until he regained his memory, he would enjoy each day as it came. This feeling of contentment was something new for him. Or maybe he'd never experienced it before.

He yawned and stretched his arms over his head, already missing the comfort of his warm bed. If not for the aroma of breakfast pulling him from his slumber, he'd probably still be cuddled down under the cozy blankets. He'd slept so soundly last night that the chirping of birds outside his bedroom window hadn't wakened him like it usually did.

Guess I needed the extra sleep, he thought, *'cause today's gonna be an exciting day.* Susan would be taking him to see the hot air balloons in Paoli. Anne was supposed to go along, but she'd come down with a bad cold and thought it would be best if she stayed home and rested. Henry and Norma had been invited to go, too, but they had a church bazaar to attend. So it would just be Eddie and Susan, but that was okay with him. Susan was a lot of fun to be with, and he looked forward to spending the day together, just the two of them. It was good to feel so lighthearted and full of anticipation. He was having more and more of those kinds of days lately, and he liked it.

Halting his thoughts, Eddie pulled open the curtains to let the morning sunlight in. The room immediately transformed, draped in the day's golden warmth, not just from the sun but also from the trees right outside the window. The autumn brilliance from their yellow leaves made his bedroom glow. Before too long, the trees would be bare, and he'd be raking up the leaves. But he looked forward to that. He enjoyed doing anything in the fresh air.

I wonder if I liked being outside before I lost my memory. Did I have a job working outdoors, or was I just a bum living on the streets?

Eddie hated the fact that he still had no memory of his past, and each day that came and went without a glimmer of his memory returning made him feel more discouraged that it might never return. If not for the warm welcome he'd received from the Baileys, he'd probably have fallen victim to depression.

Eddie's stomach growled, interrupting his thoughts. He needed to get some breakfast, and soon after that, he and Susan would head out for the day. He'd probably have so much fun he wouldn't even think about his memory loss.

Bird-in-Hand

"Are you ready for a little outing?" Meredith leaned over Levi's crib, wrapped a blanket around his squirming body, and picked him up. "We're going to see some animals at the zoo, precious baby."

Levi nuzzled her neck while she gently patted his back. He was such a good baby and a comfort to her, as well. Meredith knew it would be difficult to raise him alone, but she was determined to do it. She'd been managing financially so far, but real estate taxes would be due next spring, and that worried her. She was making enough money selling head coverings to pay for food and their basic expenses, but she wasn't sure how she could put enough extra in the bank to pay taxes.

As much as Meredith dreaded doing it, she might have to rent the house out and move in with her folks. Selling the place would be her last resort, because if she did that, she'd have no place to come back to if she found a way to make more money. Meredith didn't want to look for work outside the home until Levi had been weaned, so renting out the house might be her only option if things got any worse.

A horn honked outside, interrupting Meredith's thoughts. Dorine and her driver were there, so it was time to head for the zoo.

Meredith grabbed her lightweight jacket along with Levi's diaper bag and headed out the door.

"Are you ready for a fun day?" Dorine asked as Meredith climbed into Marsha Hubert's van.

Meredith nodded. "I don't think Levi will get much out of it, but I'm sure looking forward to this time we can be together."

Dorine gestured to Merle and Cathy. "My two kinner are excited about seeing the animals at the zoo, and I'm also looking forward to watching the hot air balloons in Paoli."

"You're not planning to take a ride in one of them are you?" Meredith questioned.

Dorine shook her head vigorously. "Ach, no! I just want to watch awhile, and then we can be on our way to the zoo."

"I've been to these hot air balloon displays before," Marsha told them. "Some of the rides you can take float you from one place to a totally new location. But if you just want to experience what it's like to go up in one, then I recommend taking a tethered ride."

"What's that?" Meredith and Dorine asked in unison.

"It's a ride that takes you up high in the balloon, but you don't really go anywhere. There's a rope that's tied from the ground up to the balloon, securing it in place," their driver explained. "I can tell you from personal experience that the view up there is breathtaking."

"That sounds exciting, but I think I'll just observe," Dorine said. "I'd be too scared to go way up there."

"I agree. All I want to do is watch." Meredith buckled Levi into a car seat then settled back for the one-hour drive.

Paoli, Pennsylvania

"Would ya just look at all those colorful balloons?" Eddie pointed upward with the exuberant look of a child opening gifts on Christmas morning.

Susan smiled. "Would you like to take a ride in one of them?"

Eddie's turquoise eyes widened. "Would that be possible? I think it'd be expensive."

"We can buy a ticket for one of the tethered rides. Those don't cost as much."

"But I don't have any money," he said.

"I'll buy your ticket. And then I'll take your picture when you go up in the balloon."

"I can't let you do that."

"Why not?"

"I wouldn't feel right about you paying, but if you're gonna buy a ticket, then you should be the one takin' the balloon ride."

Susan shook her head. "Not me. I'm keeping both of my feet planted firmly on the ground."

"Then I won't go either." Eddie tipped his head and stared up at the balloons. "I've always wondered what it'd be like to fly. Least, I think I have. I can't remember actually saying that, but way down deep inside I feel like I have."

Susan touched his arm. "Then I insist that you take a balloon ride. It might spark some special memory for you."

"You really think so?"

"It's worth a try, don't you think?"

He bobbed his head, grinning from ear to ear. "You're a nice person, Susan, and I'll always be grateful for everything you've done to help me." He reached for her hand and gave her fingers a gentle squeeze.

Heat flooded Susan's cheeks. It was great being with Eddie like this—away from the hospital and away from the house for a few hours. It was almost like they were on a date— just the two of them having fun and getting to know each other better.

"*Guck emol dutt!* Have you ever seen so many balloons all in one place?" Dorine asked when they stepped out of the van in Paoli.

Meredith shielded her eyes from the glare of the morning sun. "I am looking at that, and I see so many beautiful colors it's hard to believe!" Some of the balloons were checkered with bright yellows and reds. Others were solid, brilliant colors. But seeing them all together made it look like a rainbow of shades.

Dorine laughed as she motioned to her children, who were busy pointing and giggling. "Cathy and Merle seem to like them, too."

"I'll bet they'd like to take a ride."

"Maybe someday," Dorine said, "but right now they're too little for something like that."

"I have no desire to soar up in the air like a bird." A lump formed in Meredith's throat. "But I remember how Luke said many times that he wished he could fly."

It seemed like only yesterday that Luke had grinned and pointed skyward when a plane flew over. Meredith had always smiled at his boyish reaction. Luke had also gotten excited during geese migration. He'd mentioned many times that he wondered what it would be like to fly with those birds, as they'd watched them depart every autumn in their V-formation, heading south for the winter. Meredith, enjoying springtime like she did, became excited as she heard the distant honking, signaling the geese's return. But she had no desire to be up there flying with them.

Dorine slipped her arm around Meredith's waist, bringing her back to the present. "You still miss him something awful, don't you?"

Meredith nodded as she stroked the top of Levi's head. "But I'm thankful for this little guy who reminds me so much of his *daadi*."

Dorine smiled. "He definitely has his daddy's white-blond hair, but he gets his pale blue eyes from you, Meredith."

Meredith was about to respond, when a young woman with straight dark hair walked up to them. "Didn't I meet you at the Bird-in-Hand Farmers' Market in the spring?" she asked, smiling at Meredith.

Meredith tipped her head and studied the woman. "I–I'm not sure. My sister sells her homemade faceless dolls there. Could you have met her?"

"Is her name Laurie King?" the woman asked.

Meredith nodded. "So you've met her?"

"Yes. I bought one of her dolls, and while we were talking, you and an older woman came by the stand. I was with my sister, and we spoke to you for a few minutes."

Meredith smiled. "Oh, yes, now I remember. You were asking some questions about our Amish way of life."

"That's right." The young woman extended her hand. "My name's Susan Bailey."

"I'm Meredith, and this is my son, Levi." Meredith kissed the top of the baby's head.

"He's a beautiful boy."

"Thank you."

"I'll bet he's the apple of his daddy's eye."

Meredith blinked to keep tears from spilling over. "My husband passed away in January."

"I'm sorry to hear that," Susan said sincerely. Then she glanced up and said, "Are you here to take a balloon ride?"

"Oh, no," Meredith was quick to say. "My friend Dorine and I are taking our children to the Elmwood Park Zoo in Norristown today, and we decided to stop by on our way to see all the colorful hot air balloons."

"I'm with a friend today, too." Susan pointed to a red-and-blue balloon that was tethered to the ground and had just lifted off. "See that young man wearing the red ball cap and sunglasses, leaning over the edge of the basket, waving to everyone?"

"I—I think so," Meredith said. "But the balloon's getting higher, and it's hard to see the people inside."

"Well, my friend Eddie is taking what I believe is his first hot air balloon ride." Susan smiled and snapped a picture with the camera she held. "I'm pretty sure he's having a wonderful time."

Meredith stood watching the balloon lift higher and saw Susan's friend waving to the people on the ground. She could only imagine what it must feel like to be up there so high. That man sure looked like he was having fun.

For a split second, she thought about taking a ride, too. After all, that particular balloon was somewhat stationary, being tethered safely to the ground. From up there, it would surely give a beautiful view of Lancaster County. But the baby started to cry, so she dismissed her thoughts.

"I think Levi is hungry, so we'd better go," Meredith whispered to Dorine.

"That's fine with me, if you're sure you've seen enough," her friend replied.

"Yes, I believe so." Meredith turned to Susan and said, "It was nice seeing you again. I hope you and your friend will enjoy the rest of your day."

"You, too," Susan said, before taking another picture of her friend in the balloon. She certainly seemed excited about seeing him up there.

Meredith turned and followed Dorine back to the van, where their driver sat slurping on the last of the milk shake she'd bought from a nearby vendor. Meredith looked back one last time and giggled when the man in the balloon, slowly drifting to its highest point, waved again.

She realized he'd been waving to everyone, and he probably wasn't even looking at her, but she waved back anyway. She wished she could stay and watch the balloons a few more minutes, but Levi, who'd started crying even louder, couldn't wait any longer to eat. Besides, they really needed to be on their way to the zoo.

Eddie leaned over the edge of the basket, grinning like a child. He couldn't believe how high he was. It felt like he could see for miles and miles. The countryside was so beautiful, and the trees were awesome in their autumn glory. If Norma had come, she'd probably say that God had painted this perfect picture.

Looking out over the vibrant reds, blazing oranges, and sensational yellows that stood in contrast to the green grass and wheat-colored fields made it look as if a colorful quilt were blanketing the earth.

When the tether got to its highest point, the balloon just floated where it stopped. It seemed to Eddie as if everything else had disappeared.

He could hear the other people who'd ridden up with him in the basket talking, but it was like hearing voices that were far away. At this very moment, up there in the bird's atmosphere, he felt free.

Eddie inhaled deeply. The air felt so pure; it smelled like the wind. He felt alive and at the same time incredibly grateful that he'd had the opportunity to take this ride. This seemed like a dream come true, only he couldn't remember ever wanting to do it before.

He closed his eyes briefly, thanking God for this special day, which he knew he'd remember for a long time to come.

"So what do you think, son?" the middle-aged balloon pilot asked, clasping Eddie's shoulder.

"I—I think it's great being up here so high." Eddie looked down. He could see several cars and trucks on the roads below, winding through all that color. "Everything seems so small from way up here," he murmured. "It's pretty amazing."

"You're right about that." The pilot pointed to the ground. "Everyone down there looks like tiny specks."

Eddie nodded. The people reminded him of the little ants he'd seen scurrying back and forth across the Baileys' porch steps.

At first, when the balloon ventured higher and higher, Eddie had shouted and waved to those on the ground. Now, though, he felt humbled and could hardly talk. He didn't want this moment to end. It was as if he was somehow fulfilling a dream.

CHAPTER 6

Darby

As Eddie walked through the Baileys' living room on a Monday morning in early October, he spotted an old shutter that had been refinished and painted with an unusual design. He reached out his hand and rubbed the glossy finish, amazed at how smooth it felt.

"Ah, I see you're admiring my piece of art," Henry said, strolling into the room, wearing a straw hat with a wide brim.

Eddie nodded. "Did you make it?"

Henry shook his head. "Not hardly. Susan

and Anne bought it for me at a farmers' market some time ago."

"This is the first time I've seen it here," Eddie said. "Think I would have noticed something this nice before."

Henry chuckled. "It was in our bedroom, but Norma said it was too nice to keep where only we could enjoy it, so this morning I brought it out here."

"It's sure smooth." Eddie pursed his lips. "Whoever made it did a fine job of sanding, that's for sure."

Henry's bushy eyebrows lifted high. "You sound like you know a little something about that. Do you think you might have done some type of carpentry work before your accident?"

Eddie shrugged. "I don't know. Wish I did, but try as I might, I still can't remember anything about my life before I woke up in the hospital." He dropped his gaze to the floor. "I'm beginning to think I'll never get my memory back."

Henry clasped Eddie's shoulder and gave it a reassuring squeeze. "Just give it some time, son, and try to relax. My guess is if you try to force yourself to remember, that may do more harm than good. Why, I'll bet when you aren't even thinking about it, one day"—he snapped his fingers—"memories from your past will just pop into your head."

Eddie wished Henry was right, but did he dare hope for such a miracle?

"Just remember," Henry added, looking Eddie straight in the eyes, "Norma, the girls, and I are praying for you."

"I appreciate that." Eddie had gone to church with the Baileys every Sunday since he'd moved into their home, and he'd heard the pastor talk about prayer. He didn't remember ever going to church before moving here, but for some reason, a few of the scriptures the pastor had read seemed familiar to him. However, the worship service wasn't familiar at all. In fact, the first Sunday Eddie had gone to the Baileys' church, he'd felt kind of odd—like he didn't belong inside such a fancy building. Was it because he'd been a bum living on the streets before he'd been brought to the hospital all those months ago?

Henry gave Eddie's back a light thump. "So

what do you say? Should we head out back and rake up those leaves? After that wind last night, most of them are off the trees. The day looks like it's gonna be a beaut."

"Sure, no problem." Eddie followed Henry out the door. Once outside, he grabbed a rake and started to tackle the leaves. Inhaling a deep breath, he noticed the scent of decaying leaves as he raked them into piles. A slight breeze still blew but nothing like the howling wind they'd had overnight. The grass was green yet, like it had been over summer, but with the recent frost they'd had, it was no longer growing so fast. Soon, the days of mowing would come to an end, and not long after, as Henry had mentioned the other day, it'd be time to get the snow shovels out.

Henry was right about this day being beautiful, Eddie thought as he paused to lean on the rake handle. Looking up into the crystal sky, the color was so blue it almost hurt his eyes. This was a far cry from the last couple of mornings, when the fog had been heavy and the grass wet with dew.

"I always hate to see autumn come to an

end," Henry said, raking his own pile of leaves. "It comes and goes too quickly for me." He looked over at Eddie and smiled. "What's your favorite season?"

Eddie shrugged. "I don't really know." He looked up at the sky once more as a helicopter flew overhead and listened as the whirl of the propeller grew fainter. He thought then about the hot air balloon ride he'd taken just a month ago. It had sure been fun to be up there so high, looking down on the people below. *I wonder if I'll ever have the chance to ride in another balloon again. Or better yet, maybe an airplane.*

As Eddie raked the piles of leaves into one big mound, he stopped to look at it and thought how inviting it looked. *I wonder what Henry would think if I took a flying leap right into the middle of those leaves.*

Dismissing that thought as being too childish, Eddie reflected on how much fun he and Susan had had that day at the balloon festival. He enjoyed being with Susan so much and wished he felt free to begin a relationship with her. If he could just get his memory back, maybe he and Susan could start dating. Until then, however, he couldn't let her know how he felt, not to mention the voice inside that nagged at him relentlessly. As much as Eddie tried to ignore it, the voice kept warning: *Hold off; just wait. Don't make any hasty decisions.*

Ronks, Pennsylvania

Breakfast was over, and everyone in the King household was going about their normal routine. Nina, Stanley, Arlene, and Katie had left over an hour ago for school. Kendra was downstairs, helping Mom sort the laundry, and Laurie could hear her three-year-old brother, Owen, who was also in the basement, laughing out loud. No doubt he was amusing himself with the empty boxes stacked in the corner. Owen loved crawling inside them. Sometimes he would put several of the boxes together, like he was playing house. Once he'd even fallen asleep inside one.

Laurie's dad had left at sunup to pick up his friend Richard Zook for a ride over to

Gordonville, where they'd be looking at some Rhode Island Reds to buy. Laurie had already cleaned up the kitchen and had just stepped into the living room to join Grandma Smucker, who sat in the rocking chair, crocheting a bed covering for her great-grandson, Levi.

"How's that blanket coming along?" Laurie asked, picking up a pencil and tablet and taking a seat on the sofa across from Grandma.

Grandma smiled. "Pretty well. It should be done by the time the temperatures dip." She held up the covering for Laurie to see. "It'll be an extra coverlet for Meredith to put over little Levi when winter's upon us."

"I'm sure it'll be nice and warm for him," Laurie commented, focusing on the list she'd started.

"Looks like a nice day out there," Grandma said, glancing toward the window. "Fall is surely upon us. Did you ever see so many leaves in the yard?"

"Hmm. . ." Laurie chewed on the end of her pencil, trying to think of what all she wanted to add to her list. She and Kevin were planning to be married the first week of December, and a lot remained to get done in the coming weeks. It wasn't just the wedding either. A month after that, Laurie would be accompanying Kevin on a work-and-witness trip to Mississippi, where they'd be working in a Native American community. Her future husband had been on several missionary trips before. He'd even gone out of the country a few times. But since this would be Laurie's introduction to missionary work, Kevin had signed them up for work in the United States.

Little by little, Kevin had been orienting Laurie on what they'd be doing once they got to Mississippi. Things like taking the children to local events at a nearby church, preparing food, and helping to celebrate the children's birthdays, which were a festive occasion among the Native Americans. At times the mission also provided transportation for the elderly to doctor and dental appointments, as well as trips to town for other things.

Laurie's life was about to change, but she was excited about it. She'd be working side by side with the man she loved. She only wished everyone in her family was as exuberant as she was.

"Ah-hem."

"Sorry, Grandma. Did you say something?" Laurie's face heated as she looked up from the tablet.

"I asked how your list was coming along."

"Oh, I don't know. There's so much to do yet before the wedding, not to mention the work-and-witness trip Kevin and I will be taking."

"Maybe you should think more about this decision you've made," Grandma said. "It might not hurt to give yourself a little more time to make sure you're doing the right thing and choosing the right direction for your future."

"There's nothing for me to think about, Grandma. I love Kevin. He's a kind, caring person, and the things I've learned from him about missionary work make me love him even more. I think everyone in our family just needs to give him a chance." Laurie sighed. "I wouldn't be doing this if I didn't feel it was right. I know Kevin will be good to me, and I'll be good to him, too."

"But it seems like this is all happening rather quickly," Grandma rationalized, placing her crocheting in her lap. "Your parents had hopes of you remaining in the Amish faith."

"I know that, but—"

"Please, hear me out." Grandma's glasses had fallen to the middle of her nose, and she paused to push them back in place. "I wanted to add that the important thing is that Amish and Mennonite Christian beliefs are very much the same except for some differences in how we view the outside world. Only you can decide if becoming a missionary is the path you wish to take."

"Oh, it is, Grandma," Laurie was quick to say. "I want to spend the rest of my life with Kevin, helping others who are less fortunate and teaching them about Jesus. I know in my heart that this is the right thing for me, because I have a personal relationship with Jesus, and I feel called to work alongside Kevin in sharing the Gospel."

Grandma smiled. "I understand. Just give us all some time to adjust to this new change. It's not easy to let go—especially knowing at times you'll be far from home."

"But I'll never forget you," Laurie said with

a shake of her head. "I'll never forget any of my family."

Bird-in-Hand

Holding Levi firmly in her arms, Meredith shuffled through the fallen leaves in her backyard, enjoying the crackling sound beneath her feet. It was a lovely fall day, and she took pleasure in being outside. She thought the baby must like it, too, for he seemed so alert, making gurgling noises and turning his little head in the direction of the birds chirping and soaring overhead.

Meredith hugged her son even closer. This little guy had brought so much joy to her, as well as to the rest of her family. The other day, when Mom had come by with Owen and Katie, Meredith had laughed when Owen crawled inside an empty cardboard box in her utility room. In another few months, Levi would probably be crawling, and he might be looking for boxes to play in, too.

Meredith smiled. She couldn't imagine life now, without her precious son.

As a bird swooped down to get a drink from the birdbath, Meredith thought about the hot air balloons she and Dorine had seen in Paoli last month. *Oh, how Luke would have enjoyed taking a ride in one of those,* she thought.

Meredith could still remember the group of people she'd seen in the tethered balloon. One of them—the nurse's friend, wearing a red ball cap and sunglasses—had seemed the most excited of all, waving and shouting to the people below. It sure looked like he was having the time of his life. As the balloon rose as far as it could go, the people in the basket had looked so small she couldn't make out any of their faces. She figured from their perspective the people on the ground probably looked even smaller.

Meredith wished now that she'd taken a ride in the balloon, just to see what it was like way up there. She'd never been an adventurous person, but maybe it was time to step out of her comfort zone and start taking some chances. What those chances would be, she didn't know yet, but she'd be ready when the opportunities arose. Being afraid all the time and cautious of everything was no fun at all.

Her thoughts shifted again, thinking about Laurie and the new adventure she and Kevin would take on once they were married. Mom and Dad weren't happy about Laurie not joining the Amish faith, but they were trying to be understanding. Sometimes when grown children made a decision to do something their parents didn't agree with, they just had to let go and accept things as they were.

When Jonah pulled his horse and buggy into Meredith's yard, he spotted her walking through a pile of leaves, holding the baby in her arms. Just the sight of her caused his heart to pound. Oh, how he longed to make her his wife.

He pulled Socks up to the hitching rail, and as soon as he had him secured, he sprinted across the yard toward Meredith. *"Wie geht's?"* he called as she waved and headed toward the house.

"I'm doing okay," she said when he joined her on the porch. "How are you?"

I'm fine now that I'm here with you. "Doin' good," he replied, keeping his thoughts to himself. "Just came by to check on you and extend an invitation."

"Oh?" She tipped her head and looked up at him with questioning eyes.

"My folks and I are planning a little barbecue on Saturday night, and I was wondering if you and Levi would like to come." Jonah reached out and stroked the baby's head.

"Sure, that sounds real nice." Meredith smiled. "Can I bring anything?"

Jonah shook his head. "Just a hearty appetite, 'cause between my barbecued burgers and all the food Mom will fix, there'll be more than enough to eat." He shuffled his feet a few times, feeling like a bashful schoolboy. "Would it be okay if I came by and picked you up around four o'clock?"

"Oh, you don't have to do that. Your folks' place isn't too far from here, and I can ride over with my own horse and buggy."

"I'm sure you can, but I thought it'd be

easier for you and the baby if I gave you a ride."

Meredith didn't say anything for several seconds, but then she slowly nodded. "All right then, Levi and I will be ready for you to pick us up by four o'clock."

Jonah grinned. If everything went well on Saturday evening and his nerves didn't take over, he planned to ask Meredith if he could court her.

CHAPTER 7

Bird-in-Hand

*J*onah whistled as he flipped hamburgers on the grill. It was great having Meredith and little Levi with them tonight. He glanced up at the porch where Meredith sat on the glider, holding the baby in her arms. Mom was seated nearby in a wicker chair, with Herbie lying on the porch next to her feet. It looked as if the women were deep in conversation, and he was curious to know what they were talking about.

Maybe Mom's putting in a good word for me, Jonah thought. He'd confided in her the other day that he planned to ask Meredith if he could start courting her. Mom had smiled and said she hoped it worked out.

Tonight's the night, Jonah thought. *I just can't wait any longer.*

"Ya better watch it, Son, or you'll burn those burgers," Dad said, stepping up to Jonah and pointing at the grill. "They look pretty done to me."

"Oh, right." Jonah quickly pulled his thoughts aside and scooped the burgers onto the serving tray Mom had provided. The last thing he wanted to do was serve scorched burgers to Meredith. Tonight he wanted everything to be perfect. "Guess I had my mind on something else."

"And it doesn't take a genius to know who." Dad chuckled, nodding toward the house.

Jonah's face heated. Although he hadn't told him of his intentions tonight, he had a feeling Dad already knew. With him going over to Meredith's place so often these days, it was fairly obvious.

Dad thumped Jonah's shoulder. "Well, let's get the ladies and tell 'em it's time to eat. I can't speak for anyone else, but I'm *hungerich.*"

Jonah smiled. Smelling the meat as it cooked had made him hungry, too.

Soon they were all seated around the picnic table. Mom and Dad sat on one side and Meredith and Jonah on the other. Levi, sound asleep in his little carrier, was close to his mother. Taking a quick look around, Jonah almost felt as if Meredith and the baby were part of his family.

After their silent prayer, Mom passed around the coleslaw and potato salad she'd made earlier, and Jonah put a burger and bun on everyone's plate. There were also potato chips, some of Mom's homemade dill pickles, and Jonah's favorite—pickled eggs and red beets. It was a little chilly, but the grown-ups wore jackets, and baby Levi was bundled in a cozy-looking blanket Meredith said her grandma had made.

"Sure is a pleasant evening for a barbecue," Mom said after she'd poured everyone a cup of warm apple cider. "Right now it's pleasant because there's hardly any bugs this time of year, but it won't be long before the days will be too cold for eating outside."

"That's okay." Jonah grinned. "I can still barbecue, and we'll eat inside."

"You won't barbecue when there's snow on the ground, I hope," Meredith said, wrinkling her nose.

He shrugged his shoulders. "Probably not; although I could put the grill on the porch."

Dad shook his head. "What would be the point in you standin' outside in the cold when your mamm can cook supper in her kitchen where it's warm and toasty? You can save the barbecuing for the months with nicer weather and leave the wintertime cooking to her."

Mom looked over at Meredith with furrowed brows. "You don't have much on your plate. Don't you care for either of the salads I made?"

"Oh, it's not that. I'm just not very hungry tonight," Meredith replied.

"Jonah will probably eat your share then," Dad said, reaching for some ketchup to put on his bun. "He always eats at least two burgers."

Meredith smiled, but her face looked a bit strained. Jonah wondered if she wished she hadn't come. "Is everything all right?" he asked with concern. Jonah wasn't so sure he'd be able to eat two burgers like he usually did. All of a sudden, he wasn't real hungry either.

"I haven't been sleeping well the last few nights, and I think it's affected my appetite," Meredith explained.

"Is the boppli keeping you awake?" Mom asked, motioning to Levi, who was still asleep.

"That's only part of it," Meredith murmured. "I've been worried about my finances and wondering if I ought to put my house up for rent."

"Where would you go if you did that?" Jonah asked, wishing he could solve her problems right now.

Meredith shrugged. "Probably back home with my folks. I'm sure Luke's parents would take Levi and me in, but I'd rather not impose on them."

Jonah drew in a long breath. If he and Meredith were already courting, he'd ask her to marry him right now so she wouldn't have to worry about her finances. But now wasn't the time to speak of marriage. In just a few more months, her year of mourning would be over. In the meantime, he needed to take things slow and not rush her. But if his folks hadn't been sitting there, he'd ask Meredith if he could court her right now.

"I think we should go inside now," Jonah's mother, Sarah, said after they'd finished eating. "The sun's going down, and it's getting too chilly for the boppli to be out here."

"You're right," Meredith agreed. "I'm thinking maybe it's time for Levi and me to go home." She glanced over at Jonah.

"But we haven't had our dessert yet," Jonah said. "Mom made a couple of apple pies."

"That's right," Sarah agreed. "So why don't I take the boppli inside, and you and Meredith can sit out here awhile and watch as the sun goes down and the stars come out. After you've seen enough, you can join us in the kitchen for a piece of pie."

"That sounds nice," Meredith replied, "but I have to change Levi first. Come to think of it, I haven't taken the time to watch the stars come out in a long while." *Not since Luke died,* she thought with regret.

"I'll help clear away the dishes," Jonah said, jumping up from the table. "Then I'll grab a blanket from the house in case we get cold."

Meredith smiled. She was sure the look of pleasure on Sarah's face meant that she appreciated her son's willingness to help out.

"I'll move the grill back to the shed," Jonah's dad, Raymond, said.

"Better make sure it's cooled off good before you put it away," Jonah commented. "Remember what happened a few years ago when the Bontragers' barn burned down?"

Dad nodded. "Who could forget that? It was unfortunate that a day of celebrating turned to tragedy when Ethan Bontrager wheeled their grill into the barn when it wasn't cooled off yet."

Jonah's forehead wrinkled as he reflected on that evening. The Bontragers had been his folks' best friends when they lived in Ohio. They'd been celebrating one of their children's birthdays by having a big cookout. Everything had been going well, until a sudden thunderstorm blew in; then chaos broke loose. Everyone ran, grabbing what they could. The grill, which had still been hot, was wheeled into the barn, and they ended up continuing the party inside the house. In the end, they lost their barn and all its contents, including tools, buggies, two horses, and a milking cow, all because they hadn't let the grill cool.

Goose bumps erupted on Jonah's arm, imagining such a disaster happening to his folks. Thankfully, no one in the Bontrager family had been hurt that night, but having seen what had taken years to acquire go up in smoke because of a careless decision, Jonah knew the little reminder he'd given his dad could do no harm.

"It's all good," Dad said, as he pulled the grill toward the shed. "There's no heat left at all."

While Jonah's dad headed for the shed, Meredith, carrying Levi's infant seat, followed Jonah and Sarah up to the house. Once inside, Meredith fed the baby and changed his diaper.

When she was done, she set his carrier in the living room, where Sarah and Jonah had gone after the dishes were done. Raymond joined them a few minutes later.

"Should we go outside now?" Jonah asked, lightly touching Meredith's arm.

Meredith looked at Sarah. "Are you sure you don't mind keeping an eye on Levi?"

Sarah shook her head. "Not at all."

Meredith, feeling a bit apprehensive about leaving the baby, said, "If he starts fussing and you can't get him settled down, just come and get me."

"I'm sure he'll be fine. If he does wake up, it'll give me a good excuse to hold him." Sarah motioned to the door. "Now you and Jonah go out and enjoy watching the stars."

Jonah grabbed a crocheted afghan from the back of the sofa and held the door for Meredith. When they stepped onto the porch, Meredith's breath caught in her throat. Glowing splashes of color—pink, orange, and red—spread across the sky as the sun sank slowly into the west. She stood on the porch, watching until the sun and its glorious shine disappeared. Suddenly, a multitude of stars peeked out under the dark night sky.

"Sure is a beautiful night, isn't it?" Jonah whispered, leaning close to Meredith.

"Jah." She shivered, not knowing if the chill she felt was from the cool evening breeze or from Jonah's breath blowing softly against her ear.

"Should we stay here on the porch or walk out to the picnic table to watch for falling stars?" Jonah asked, draping the afghan across her shoulders.

"Let's go out to the picnic table. I think we'll be able to see the stars better from there."

Jonah led the way, and once they were seated on the picnic bench, Meredith turned to face him. "Luke and I used to sit outside and watch for falling stars. It was a special thing we liked to do. We did some stargazing our last night together."

Jonah placed his hand gently on her arm. "You still miss him, don't you?"

She nodded. "I wake up some mornings and expect to see Luke lying there beside me. Sometimes I dream that I look out the window and see him walking up the driveway. But just as he nears the house, he suddenly disappears."

"It's hard to lose someone you love," Jonah said. "I know Luke's memory will always be with you, but do you think you might ever find room in your heart to love again?"

Meredith sat several seconds before she replied. "I don't know—maybe."

"I care for you, Meredith," Jonah murmured. "And I—well, I was wondering if you'd be willing to let me court you."

Meredith wasn't sure what to say. She cared for Jonah, too. He was a good friend, but could she ever love him the way she had Luke? If Luke could reach down from heaven and tell her what to do, would he give his approval for her to be courted again?

She looked up at the starry sky, and when she spotted a falling star, a lump formed in her throat. Could this be a sign from Luke that it was okay for her to move on without him and perhaps take the next step to continue her life—a new life with Jonah?

"Meredith, have I said too much? Is it too soon for me to be talking about us courting?" Jonah asked.

After seeing the falling star, Meredith drew in a deep breath and released it slowly. "No, Jonah, it's not too soon. I'd be honored to have you court me."

Jonah reached for her hand, surprised at how warm it felt. "I'm the one who's honored."

Darby

"Did you ever see such a beautiful night sky?" Susan asked as she took a seat beside Eddie on the lawn swing in the Baileys' backyard. Norma, Henry, and Anne had already gone to bed, but Susan had said she wasn't tired, and when Eddie said he wasn't either, she'd suggested they go outside and gaze at the stars.

"You're right," he said, tilting his head back to look at the sky. "Some of the stars are so bright it seems like you could almost reach out and touch 'em."

"Ever since Anne and I were little girls, we've enjoyed watching the stars. It's fun to search for the Big and Little Dippers and all the other constellations. But it's not only that. Watching the stars this time of the year holds a special place in my heart."

"What do you mean?" Eddie asked, his curiosity piqued.

"Well, as far back as I can remember, sitting outside on a cool October night is something my family did every year. That is, up until our parents were killed. Anne and I were teenagers when it happened." Susan paused, and her voice faltered. "But before their deaths, every fall we'd pick a night such as this and call it our 'make a wish night.' At sunset, Dad would put a log on to burn in the barbecue pit in our backyard, and we'd wait until the coals turned to embers. By then the sky was totally dark, like it is now. Mom made hot chocolate, and we'd sit side by side and watch the sky, holding our mugs with fingers sticky from the marshmallows we'd roasted." She paused again, her voice growing lower. "All year long I'd think of one special wish, and I'd save it for that special night. Then, when I'd see a falling star, I'd make my wish. Of course, even back then I knew making wishes was just for fun. From the time we were little,

Dad and Mom taught Anne and me about the importance of prayer and how we should ask God to meet our needs."

"And has He?" Eddie asked.

She nodded slowly. "Even though Mom and Dad were taken from us, Anne and I have never done without. Grandma and Grandpa make sure of that, and we're grateful to them."

Eddie reached for Susan's hand as they stared up at the velvety blackness above. Suddenly, out of the darkness, a shooting star streaked across the sky, causing him to shiver. A strange feeling came over him; he felt like he'd done this before with someone else—a young woman, perhaps. He felt goose bumps rising on his arms. Was it the strange feeling of having stargazed with someone before, or was it because Susan's soft hand rested securely in his?

"Did you see that shooting star, Merrie?" he murmured.

Susan's hand slipped away from his. "Merrie? Who's Merrie, Eddie?"

"I don't know." He shook his head slowly, feeling even more confused. "I don't know why, but I feel like that shooting star has something to do with my past. If I could only remember who I'd seen it with, it might give me a clue as to who I am."

CHAPTER 8

Ronks

"Ach, Meredith, what a surprise! I didn't expect to see you this morning," Luann said when she opened the door and found Meredith on the porch with Levi in her arms.

Meredith smiled. "I've been meaning to come by and tell you my news, but Levi's been fussy all week, and I didn't want to take him out."

"What news is that?" Luann asked, reaching out to stroke the baby's soft cheek.

"Jonah and I are going to start courting."

Luann gasped. "When was this decided?"

"Last Saturday Levi and I were invited to the

Millers' for a barbecue, and later that evening Jonah asked if he could begin courting me."

Luann sucked in her breath. "Ach, Meredith, are you sure about this? I mean, do you love Jonah?"

"Not in the same way I did Luke, but Jonah's a wonderful man, and I'll get to know him even better when we start courting. If we should end up getting married someday, I'm sure he'll be a good daed to Levi."

Luann stood a few seconds, unsure of what to say. She knew Jonah and Meredith were friends and that he'd gone over to her place many times to help out, but she hadn't realized things were getting serious between them.

"You're awfully quiet, Mom. What do you think about this?"

"Well, you took me by surprise. I hadn't realized your relationship with Jonah was anything more than friendship, but if being courted by him will make you happy, then you have my blessing." Luann paused, and her forehead wrinkled. "I hope you won't agree to marry him too soon, though, or that your decision will be based on your financial needs."

Meredith shook her head. "I know Jonah would be a good provider, but that's not the reason I agreed to let him court me. I care very much for Jonah, and he's good with the boppli."

"So have you made this decision more for the baby than yourself?"

"Not more; it's just one of the reasons."

"Do Sadie and Elam know about this?" Luann questioned.

"No, not yet. It'll be hard telling Luke's folks that Jonah and I will be courting, but I know I have to. I wouldn't want them to hear about it from someone else. It would hurt them deeply."

Gordonville, Pennsylvania

"Wie geht's?" Sadie asked when she stepped into the bookstore and spotted Sarah Miller browsing through a stack of cookbooks.

Sarah smiled. "I'm doing well. How are you?"

"Doin' as well as can be expected, I guess."

"Have you heard Meredith and Jonah's news?" Sarah asked.

Sadie's eyebrows arched. "What news is that?"

"They're going to start courting."

Sadie's mouth dropped open, and her heart pounded so hard she felt like her chest might explode. "W—when was this decided?"

"Last Saturday Jonah asked Meredith if he could court her." Sarah smiled widely. "Raymond and I think the world of Meredith, and we're happy Jonah's found such a wonderful woman. If they were to marry someday, it would mean so much to have someone as special as Meredith for our daughter-in-law."

Sadie gripped the edge of the bookshelf for support. Learning that Meredith and Jonah were planning to court was surprising enough, but the fact that Meredith hadn't said anything to her and Elam about it was disappointing and hurtful. Didn't their daughter-in-law think they had the right to know? How long was she planning to keep this news from them?

Sadie looked at Sarah, unable to form any words. Did Sarah expect her to be happy about Jonah and Meredith courting? She knew what a wonderful daughter-in-law the Millers would be getting if Meredith ended up marrying their son. But it didn't seem fair. Meredith was Sadie's daughter-in-law, and Levi was *her* grandson. This year had been difficult enough for her and Elam with the loss of their son. Sadie had been hoping the family's support would be enough for Meredith and that she would give herself more time before agreeing to let someone court her. *Time, though, for who?* she wondered. *Would I be happy about anyone courting Meredith, or is it just Jonah I don't approve of?*

Jonah seemed like a nice enough man, and he would probably be good to Meredith and Levi. But if Meredith should marry him, things would be different, and she might end up pulling away from Sadie and Elam. That would hurt so much—especially if they didn't get to see Levi very often.

"Sadie, I'm so sorry," Sarah said with a look of pity in her eyes. "I wasn't thinking, blurting that out. I should have let Meredith tell you."

Sadie squared her shoulders, determined not to let Sarah know how she really felt. "It's okay," she murmured. "I'm glad you told me."

Sarah looked like she might say something

more, but Sadie turned and hurried from the bookstore before the tears welling in her eyes spilled onto her cheeks.

Bird-in-Hand

Jonah and his dad had been working hard in the buggy shop all morning, and at noontime, Jonah was more than ready to take a break.

"Let's get this wheel put on Aaron Raber's buggy, and then we can go up to the house for lunch," Dad said.

"That's fine. Guess my stomach can wait a few more minutes," Jonah said with a grin.

As they worked together, Jonah told his dad about a house he was interested in buying. "It's only a few miles from here," he said. "So if I get the place, I can probably ride my scooter on nice days to get to work."

"Are you thinking of puttin' an offer on it now, or will you wait to see how things work out between you and Meredith?" Dad asked.

"I think I ought to buy it now 'cause it might

not be there in a few months," Jonah replied. "Besides, if I get the place now, then I'll have some time to fix it up. I want things to work out for me and Meredith, probably more than you realize. But even if it doesn't, I'd still like to buy a place of my own. Maybe someday I'll have a wife and family, like I've always hoped for."

"That's good thinking, Son." Dad gave Jonah's shoulder a tight squeeze. He headed across the room to his workbench. "Think I'd better look for a bigger wrench." He'd no sooner reached for the wrench when he let out a yelp. "Yikes! I think something bit my hand."

Jonah set the wheel on the floor and hurried across the room. "Better let me take a look at that."

"I think it was a spider," Dad said, looking toward the tool he'd dropped, while rubbing his hand. "I've been meaning to spray the shop after seeing several webs but haven't gotten around to it yet. It's warm in here with the woodstove burning, and since it's getting cooler outside, I've noticed more webs showing up in the shop."

"You might be right, but don't worry about

that right now." Jonah took hold of his dad's hand. "Let's hope it wasn't a black widow." Taking a closer look, he noticed how quickly the area of the bite had begun to redden and swell. "You'd better get inside and put some ice on that bite while I go to the phone shack and call our driver. The sooner you see a doctor, the better it'll be." Jonah knew that, while usually not deadly, the bite from a black widow spider could be serious.

The wrench still lay on the workbench where Dad had dropped it, and sure enough, on a post right by the table, a shiny black spider was repairing its damaged web.

A quick look around revealed numerous webs up in the rafters and some spun between several unused tools. Jonah picked up a hammer and stood watching, taking in the spider's details. Just as the eight-legged menace came out of its web and crawled across the tabletop surface, Jonah smacked it with the hammer.

Dashing from the shop to the phone shack, he mentally pictured the red, hourglass shape on the spider's belly. He was positive that Dad had been bitten by a black widow spider.

Darby

"Sure will be glad when we get this done," Henry said as he and Eddie chopped a stack of firewood.

Eddie stopped long enough to wipe his sweaty forehead. "Guess we can be glad it's not hot and humid like it was this summer."

Henry grinned. "Always did like the fall for that very reason."

Eddie went back to chopping, while Henry stacked the wood into a pile under a lean-to near the shed. When they were halfway done, Henry removed the straw hat on his head and waved it in front of his face. "Don't know about you, but I'm hungry. Let's go inside and see if Norma has lunch ready yet."

"Sounds good to me." Eddie set his axe aside and followed Henry toward the house.

They found Norma in the kitchen, stirring a pot of soup. Eddie sniffed the air. "That sure smells good. What kind of soup did you make?"

"It's lentil with chunks of ham, potatoes, carrots, and onions." Norma smiled. "The vegetables are from Henry's garden, of course."

"Is the soup about ready to eat?" Henry asked, moving over to the sink to wash his hands.

"Yes it is, and as soon as you hang up your hat, we can eat."

Eddie joined Henry at the sink and watched as the older man moved slowly across the room to hang his straw hat on a wall peg near the back door. Eddie had seen Henry wear that hat many times before, but for some reason, seeing it now made him think he might have seen a hat like that before.

Shaking the idea aside, he thought about how he and Henry had been working hard all morning and how Henry's muscles were probably sore. Eddie, on the other hand, felt pretty good. He figured all the physical therapy, plus working around there, had built up his muscles. He'd noticed the other morning when he looked in the mirror that his arms were really toning up. If things kept going as well as they had, he'd be done with therapy in the next few weeks. Now if he could just get his memory back, he'd be good as new.

Guess I'd better accept the fact that my memory may never return, he thought as he finished washing his hands. *And if that's the case, then I'll need to come up with some way to support myself. Can't stay here with the Baileys forever.*

"Come on, Eddie. Take a seat." Henry pulled out a chair at the table.

After everyone was seated, Henry led in prayer. "Heavenly Father, we thank You for this good-smelling soup my wife prepared and for the beautiful fall weather. I also want to thank You for bringing Eddie into our home, and we appreciate all the help he's given us. Be with Anne and Susan at the hospital today, and give them the strength they need to do their jobs. In Jesus' name we ask, amen."

A lump formed in Eddie's throat. These kind people felt like family. Even with all that had happened to him, he was truly blessed.

"Here you go," Norma said, handing Eddie a bowl of soup.

"Thanks. If it looks as good as it smells, then I'm in for a treat."

"Oh, I can guarantee it'll be good," Henry said, smacking his lips. "My wife's lentil soup is the best there is."

Norma smiled and gave Eddie the basket of crackers, followed by a tray full of sliced turkey and cheddar cheese. "Oh, my, I forgot to get out the apples I had sliced. Those always go so well with cheese." Going to the refrigerator, Norma laughed when she paused to glance out the kitchen window. "I see George out there. He's hopping all over your stack of firewood, Henry. Why, I'll bet that little critter is looking for something to eat."

"You're probably right," Henry agreed.

"We'll have to save him a treat from our lunch." Eddie smiled. Even that little squirrel had become special to him.

As they ate they talked about the church social coming up, and Norma described some of the craft items she was making that would be auctioned off. "The money our women's missionary society makes from the benefit auction will go to help some of our missionaries in Africa."

"Maybe there's something I could make to

donate," Eddie said. "I'm just not sure what it could be."

"How about helpin' me make some wooden birdhouses?" Henry suggested. "I usually make several whenever we have a benefit auction, and they've always gone for a pretty good price."

"If you'll show me what to do, I'll be glad to help. Maybe if I get good enough, I can make a feeder for little George."

Henry grinned. "Don't think it'll take much to show you. From what I've seen, you've caught on pretty fast to everything I've asked you to do since you moved here."

"That's right," Norma chimed in. "You're not only a hard worker, but you're smart."

Eddie's face heated. It was nice to be appreciated, but it embarrassed him, too.

"What time will Susan be home today?" he asked, needing to change the subject.

"She left at the crack of dawn," Norma said. "So she'll probably be here around three."

"Susan mentioned the two of us going over to the park so we could walk through the fallen leaves," Eddie said.

"That's my Susan." Norma smiled. "Always

did like to tromp around in the leaves during the fall."

Henry reached for a piece of cheese and put it between two crackers. "I remember one year, Susan and Anne raked up a big pile of leaves in our backyard just so they could jump in the middle of 'em. Susan said she liked to hear the crackle of the dried leaves."

Eddie nodded. "She told me the same thing last week when we were raking up some leaves. It almost seemed like she was making a game of it."

"I wouldn't be surprised if that was the case," Norma interjected. "She was probably pretending she was a young girl again. I can still hear both girls giggling way back then. They'd come up out of the pile with leaves stuck in their hair. Yes, it was good ole plain, simple fun."

"Whelp, I love to reminisce, and maybe we can do more of that this evening," Henry said, pulling a gold pocket watch from his pants pocket. "But I think we oughta get back outside and finish chopping the rest of that wood, don't you, Eddie? We can take a few of these crackers out for George, too."

Eddie stayed sitting, staring at the pocket watch. He could feel his heart hammering in his chest. There was something about Henry's watch that seemed familiar to him. Could he have had a watch like that at some time? If so, was the watch somehow special to him?

Norma touched Eddie's arm. "Are you all right? You've had a very strange look on your face ever since Henry took the watch out of his pocket."

"I think I may have had a watch like that sometime in my past," Eddie murmured.

"Really?" Henry leaned closer. "Think hard, Eddie. Think about the pocket watch you used to have and where it came from."

Eddie sat quietly, eyes riveted on the watch, trying to recall having had one of his own. Suddenly he jumped out of his seat and shouted, "I think I know my name. It's Luke!"

About the Author

New York Times bestselling author Wanda E. Brunstetter became fascinated with the Amish way of life when she first visited her husband's Mennonite relatives living in Pennsylvania. Wanda and her husband, Richard, live in Washington State but take every opportunity to visit Amish settlements throughout the States, where they have many Amish friends. Wanda and her husband have two grown children and six grandchildren. In her spare time, Wanda enjoys photography, ventriloquism, gardening, beachcombing, and having fun with her family.

Visit Wanda's website at www.wandabrunstetter .com, where you can learn more about her books and contact her.

Other books by Wanda E. Brunstetter

Adult Fiction
The Half-Stitched Amish Quilting Club

KENTUCKY BROTHERS SERIES
The Journey
The Healing
The Struggle

BRIDES OF LEHIGH CANAL SERIES
Kelly's Chance
Betsy's Return
Sarah's Choice

INDIANA COUSINS SERIES
A Cousin's Promise
A Cousin's Prayer
A Cousin's Challenge

SISTERS OF HOLMES COUNTY SERIES
A Sister's Secret
A Sister's Test
A Sister's Hope

BRIDES OF WEBSTER COUNTY SERIES
Going Home
Dear to Me
On Her Own
Allison's Journey

DAUGHTERS OF LANCASTER COUNTY SERIES
The Storekeeper's Daughter
The Quilter's Daughter
The Bishop's Daughter